Odd Bird Out

Helga Bansch

GECKO PRESS

It's said that ravens make poor parents, but Robert's were first-rate. They fed their fledglings, groomed their plumage, told them bedtime tales, and taught them all a raven needs to know.

"But I'll groom my own plumage, thank you," said Robert.

For a raven, Robert was downright chirpy:
chirpy in the egg, chirpy as a chick, and chirpy
as he flew through flight school.

Robert was happy as a lark and wanted all the ravens to share his enthusiasm. He adored dancing and dressing up. He cracked jokes and sang…

"Come fly with me—"

But dear oh dear, the creaky, croaky cawing!
Didn't he know he was out of tune…

...that his jokes were juvenile...

…that the appropriate, the prescribed,
the only possible clothing for a raven, was black?

After all, ravens knew best: what to wear, how to sing
and who to dance with. They knew precisely what was
proper, what was fun…and what was not.
It was proper to make fun of Robert.
But he simply went on being Robert.

On concert night, appearing as a peacock,
he belted out his raucous peacock song.
The ravens were fed up to their beady black eyeballs.

"Scram! Skedaddle! You're a scandal,"
they squawked. "Now scoot!"

Sadly Robert packed his bag.
He farewelled his family.
He flew far away.

When he could flap no further, he flopped in a tree.
He sang himself a lonely song.

A bird turned up to listen. Then another and another. Flocks of
birds alit and listened. "More! More! Encore!" they cried.
That fired him up. Robert was so pleased he sang them another
song. He spun a yarn and served up a joke. He switched his
clothes at the drop of a hat. The birds were enchanted.
They cheered and clapped.

Robert was radiant. This was the life.

He toured about in his finest feathers.
His performing career took flight.

Meanwhile, back on the branch…
It was quiet. It was calm. No one confounded the
concerts with cracked notes or quirky footwork.
There were no jarring jokes, no silly stories.
There were birds in black as far as the eye could see.
The music was nice, and there was no cawing, but
really, they wondered, should life be so boring?

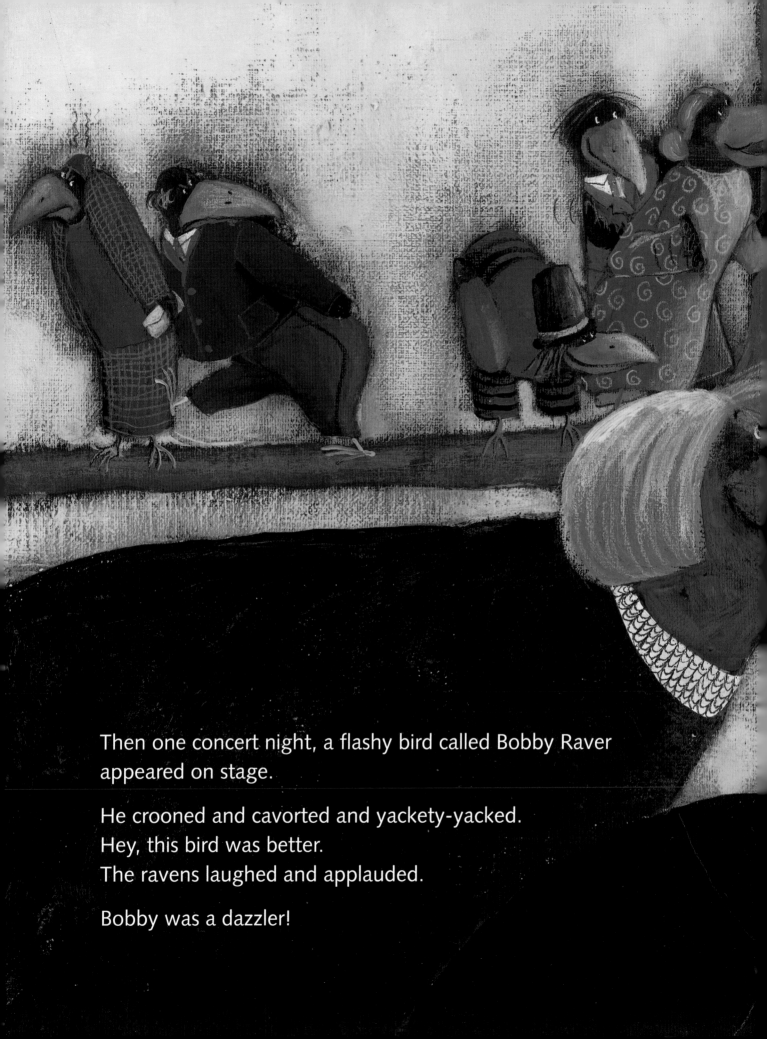

Then one concert night, a flashy bird called Bobby Raver
appeared on stage.

He crooned and cavorted and yackety-yacked.
Hey, this bird was better.
The ravens laughed and applauded.

Bobby was a dazzler!

Bobby became a star of the tree. The ravens would dress up for his concerts in the most outrageous, outlandish plumage.

Funny though—Bobby reminded them of someone.
Who could it be?

But that was Bobby's secret.